RODEO RON

AND HIS
MILKSHAKE COWS

by ROWAN CLIFFORD

ALFRED A. KNOPF   NEW YORK

Rodeo Ron moseyed into the little town of
Cavity, riding atop a bright red cow.
Following behind, nose to tail, nose to tail,
nose to tail, came three more cows.

The first, she was as yellow as
a field of sun-ripened corn.
The second was as blue
as a cloudless sky. And
the third was as green as
a fresh spring meadow.

The town's children came running right up. With every step, they let rip the biggest, fattest, wettest burps Ron had ever heard.

BURP!

BURP!

BURP!

BURP!

BURP!

"Hey, mister," they belched. "How come your cows are such funny colors?"

BURP!

BURP!

"Well," said Ron, "Red's red 'cause she eats nothing but strawberries.
Blue's blue 'cause she eats nothing but blueberries,
and Yellow there, she eats nothing but bananas."

"What about the green one, mister?"
"Well, I'll give you a clue," said Ron. "Do you like milk?"

"COW JUICE?"

"YEUCH!" squealed the kids.
"No, sir! This town only drinks
Frothy and Fruity's sodas.
You've got to try one!"

Inside the soda bar, everybody, from little old ladies to teeny little babies, was burping nonstop. And everybody had dirty brown stumps instead of bright, white smiles.

BURP!

BURP!

BURP!

BURP!

BURP!

Two brothers,
Frothy and Fruity,
stood behind the bar,
identical, except that one's mustache
pointed up and the other's pointed down.
"What's your poison, mister?" they growled.
"Orange!" shouted the kids.
"Orange it is," said Rodeo Ron.

Into a shaker, Frothy poured

orange syrup,

a shovel of sugar,

and another of bicarbonate
of soda—extra fizzy.

On went the lid, and Frothy began
to shake, and belch—so loudly that
Ron had to hold on to his hat.
Frothy slid the soda down the bar.

Rodeo Ron took a big, long gulp.
Before he could stop himself,
he let out the biggest burp of his life.

BURP!

"Hot diggity dang!" he cried.

"No wonder there's not a
white tooth in town!
It's soooooooo sweet!"

"Hey, nobody criticizes our sodas, mister!" belched Fruity.
"Yeah, unless you can do better," belched Frothy.
"I reckon I can," said Ron.
"Then I reckon you've got yourself a shake-off, mister!"

As soon as they heard the word "shake-off," the townsfolk
charged outside. The sheriff pushed his way to the front
and called out the rules: "There are four flavors;
you shake, and the kids judge."

A ripple of excited burps rose from the crowd.

Frothy and Fruity got out their chemicals and carbonates, their sugars and syrups.

Rodeo Ron pulled on his grippiest rodeo glove.

"STRAWBERRY!"
hollered the sheriff.

Frothy and Fruity sprang into action.
They poured their syrups and sugars.
They shook, they rattled,
they burped with excitement.

Meantime, Rodeo Ron
leaped astride Red
and just sat there.

BURP!

BURP!

"BORING!" said the kids. But then . . .

. . . with a huge leap,

Red shot into the air!
She bucked . . .

. . . and she bronked, she shivered and she shook, and she went

SHAKE! **SHAKE!** **SHAKE!**

Down leaped Ron and milked the frothiest, fruitiest, strawberriest milkshake anybody had ever tasted. The judges called out:

"One-nil to Rodeo Ron!"

Frothy and Fruity fizzled with rage.

"BANANA!" hollered the sheriff.
The brothers shook harder than they'd ever shaken before,
and the harder they shook, the louder they burped.

Meantime, Rodeo Ron jumped
astride Yellow and just sat there.

"BORING!" said the kids.
Suddenly, with a huge leap,
Yellow shot into the air!
She bucked . . .

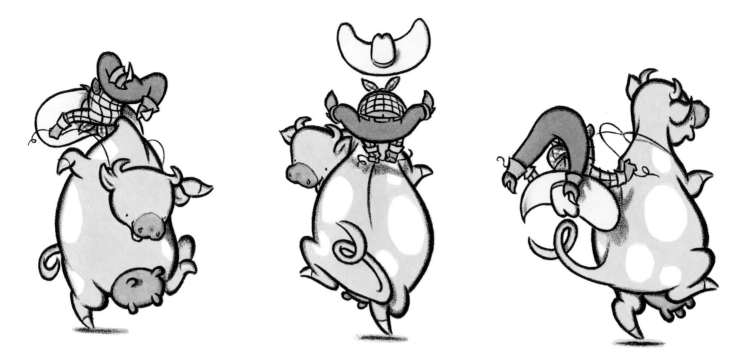

. . . and she bronked, she shivered and she shook, and she went

Down leaped Ron and milked the frothiest, fruitiest, bananariest milkshake anybody had ever tasted. The judges called out:

"Two-nil to Rodeo Ron!"

The brothers shook with rage.

Just as soon as
the sheriff hollered,
"BLUEBERRY!"
the brothers were off,
shaking like they'd never shaken before,
burping like they'd never burped before.

All the while, Ron sat quietly astride Blue.

"BORING!" said the kids.
Suddenly, with a huge leap,
Blue shot into the air! She bucked . . .

BURP!

BURP!

BURP!

BURP!

. . . and she bronked, she shivered and she shook, and she went

Down leaped Ron and milked the frothiest, fruitiest, blueberriest milkshake anybody had ever tasted. The judges called out:

"Three-nil to Rodeo Ron!"

"What?!" screamed the brothers.
"Ain't nobody makes a drink as frothy and fruity as ours!"

And before the sheriff could even call out
the last flavor, Fruity leaped onto Frothy's back
like he was one of Rodeo Ron's cows.
Well, they bucked . . .

BURP!

BURP!

BURP!

. . . and they bronked, they shivered and they shook, and they went

Louder and louder and louder and . . .

All that was left of Frothy and Fruity
was their mustaches, one pointing up
and the other pointing down.
"Holy coyote!" cried Rodeo Ron. "I guess
that was just one burp too many."

No sooner had the dust settled than one of the kids
piped up, "What about the green cow, mister?
What flavor's she?

MINT, LIME, KIWI?"

BURP!

To the townsfolk's surprise,
Rodeo Ron didn't jump onto her back.
No, he just set to, and into a glass he milked
the frothiest, creamiest, whitest milk you ever did see.

Sip by sip, the whole of Cavity tasted it.
"Why, that's the finest drink ever!" they said.

And it was, too. As the days went
by, a change came over Cavity.
Little by little, tooth by tooth,
the townsfolk got back
their bright, white smiles.

BURP!

What's more, nobody ever burped again.
Well, maybe once or twice, but they always said "pardon."

For Ally, Ellie, and Augy

THIS IS A BORZOI BOOK PUBLISHED BY ALFRED A. KNOPF

Copyright © 2005 by Rowan Clifford.

All rights reserved under International and Pan-American Copyright Conventions. Published in the United States by Alfred A. Knopf, an imprint of Random House Children's Books, a division of Random House, Inc., New York, and simultaneously in Canada by Random House of Canada Limited, Toronto.
Distributed by Random House, Inc., New York. Originally published in Great Britain in 2005 by The Bodley Head, an imprint of Random House Children's Books.

KNOPF, BORZOI BOOKS, and the colophon are registered trademarks of Random House, Inc.

Library of Congress Cataloging-in-Publication Data
Clifford, Rowan.
Rodeo Ron and his milkshake cows / Rowan Clifford. — 1st American ed.
p.   cm.
SUMMARY: Rodeo Ron rides into town in the company of four colorful cows and challenges the soda bar owners to a "shake-off" of milkshakes against soft drinks.
ISBN 0-375-83195-9 (trade) — ISBN 0-375-93195-3 (lib. bdg.)
[1. Soft drinks—Fiction. 2. Milkshakes—Fiction. 3. Milk—Fiction. 4. Cows—Fiction.
5. Nutrition—Fiction. 6. Cowboys—Fiction.]   I. Title.
PZ7.C62224Ro 2005
[E]—dc22
2004015391

www.randomhouse.com/kids

MANUFACTURED IN CHINA
May 2005
10 9 8 7 6 5 4 3 2 1
First American Edition